The Best of

Burnham Book Festival

2022

Introduction
Jonathan Pinnock

Welcome to the very first Burnham Book Festival Anthology! In these stories and poems, you'll find all sorts, from dragons and demons to pigs with superpowers and even a guest appearance from the grim reaper himself. There's humour, there's sadness and there's good and evil slugging it out yet again, head to head. There really is something for everyone to enjoy here.

Sending a story or poem into a literary competition is a pretty scary thing to do. After all, you're giving a little bit of yourself to a bunch of complete strangers to decide if they like the look of it or not. You might be shortlisted. You might even win something. But you might also get rejected, and that can be pretty disheartening.

However, if you're interested in becoming a writer at any level, the single most important skill you need to develop is learning how to deal with rejection. You need to learn how to shrug, say "never mind", and then crack on with the next one.

So congratulations to all the shortlisted writers and winners whose work appears within these covers. All of us who read your work were bowled over by your imagination and talent, and you should be very proud. We're as excited to see this anthology in print as you are.

And to those of you who didn't make it this time, make sure you come back and have another go next time. Don't, whatever you do, give up.

Poetry

Under 11 Poetry

The Meaning of Life

Florence Griffiths

Here I am, running across the battlefield,
Holding tightly the gun I wield,
Only thinking about my wife,
Hoping that she is not in strife,
Sweat is pouring down my head,
And I am leaping over the dead,
I am reaching out to cock my gun,
And suddenly a cloud is covering the sun,
We are all clambering into the trench,
Sitting, cold beside the French,
I am muttering under my breath,
I fear now something worse than death,
That I will never again see my family,
Then life would not mean much to me.

Wow that Cheetah

Mia Shore

Wow that cheetah
runs so fast,
He runs up and down
the long cheetah path.

Wow that cheetah
huge sharp claws,
running jumping and
panting on his paws.

Wow that cheetah
Nice black spots,
on the tummy, leg
wow that's lots.

Wow that cheetah
Long sharp teeth,
Soft, cuddly fur
I wonder what lies beneath.

Wow that cheetah
So fast and great,
So lovely, soft
And they will never be late.

Love

Maya Makin & Caoimhe McGuire

Cake
Top Shelf
My Fridge
The Kitchen

14th February 2022

Dear Cake,

My love for you is not fake,
You really are my favourite bake,
My love for you is so true,
You brought a smile when I was blue,

Every bite I take from you,
Is such a satisfying chew,
You never last very long,
But buying you was not wrong,

When I saw you in the shop,
My shopping bag I did drop,
For when I saw you standing there,
I needed you for my welfare,

Clutching you with quite some grip,
And trying hard not to trip,
I ran on home, forgot the car,
Oh, my precious, I ran so far!

As I held you in my fingertips,
And brought you closer to my lips,
Smiling I stroked you tenderly,
And whispered to you endlessly,

"I love you cake,
Make no mistake,
If I left you my heart would break,
I cannot bear being apart,
Cake, you are an edible art"

Finally I took a slice,
But I knew one piece would not suffice,
Though only one I did take,
From you, my beloved cake,

After placing you in my mouth,
I swallowed you and sent you south,
You were a true taste sensation,
And were a cause for celebration.

Yours truly,

Valentine xx

The Lion Popstar

Alicia Vicary

There once was a lion called Oscar
Who wanted to be a popstar.
He practised from dusk till dawn
Until he'd get so tired he'd yawn.

His voice sounded a bit gruff
Yet he thought it was good enough
He wanted to make his family proud
And show the Savannah he could be so loud.

He sang a song and, to his surprise,
The whole Savannah heard him and cried.
They thought he was brilliant and cheered as he sung,
Oscar's life as a popstar had only just begun!

Night of the City

Freida Boyer

The moonlight is on.
Glowing street lamps flicker like candlelight,
Ghostly birds swoop and fly over buildings,
Shadows are watching me.

Yellow eyes are glaring.
Tip-toeing around me like spies,
My growing pupils darting in every direction;
What's behind me?

City noises in my ears:
A fire engine is ringing a road ahead.
One stream of red in the darkness;
Someone in trouble.

My toes burning cold.
The wind speaks softly through my fingers,
My bones are shaking underneath.
The trees are waving at me.

The buildings are sleeping.
All weary flowers are tightly shut,
Only one tired car winding home,
Ignoring the church's lonely chimes.

My Fathers' Day Poem

Charlie Neilson-Pritchard

I don't want
To write a poem
It's boring

Poems are for
Old men like you
And Shakespeare

This is my poem
I hope you like it

I am Just a Little Girl (Anne Frank)

Evellyn Farnham

Love.
Love is something we all need.

Believe.
Believe this will stop soon.

Trust.
Trust everyone has good inside of them.

I am just a little girl living in this war.
Life is quite hard to enjoy.
I trust everyone around me even though I don't know them well.
But we all have to trust to play our part in this world.
We must believe that people are really good at heart.
Even though we don't know who they are.
Some people find it hard to show it but I know everyone has it.
We only live life once.
I am just a little girl living in this war.
But in spite of everything - I still believe that people are really good at heart.

11 to 15 Poetry

The Magic Box

George Pacheco

I will put in the box,

A sweet sound of the euphonium,
A rugby fan cheering on their team,
A bite of the hottest chicken wings.

I will put in the box,

The mud of the premier league ball,
The sound of a ball hitting a baseball bat,
A sip of the best Vodka.

I will put in the box,

The boom of a bomb hitting the ground,
The ooze of the fuel of a car,
The shell of a AK47.

I will put in the box,

The hiss of an elephant,
The roar of the King of The Jungle, a lion,
The bang of a gorilla hitting its chest.

The hinges are made from the tusk of an elephant.

The worst are in the corners.

The colour is camouflage.

My box is fashioned with gun steel and bamboo and the crystals of the ocean.

I will ride my box,

to the highest hills in the world.

I will end up at the Amazon Rainforest.

The colour of parts of the Earth.

Saving Lives

Imogen Elstob

We never saw it coming
We didn't believe it was real
We all ignored the warnings
We all said "no big deal"
We thought we were untouchable
Those things won't happen to us
It's fine, it's fine, wait - oh my god
And that day
The world
Just
Stopped.

BAM BAM BAM
What's happening?
You've got to stay at home
Everything is shutting down
There's nowhere for you to go
Don't socialise
Go out once a day
And only if it's unavoidable
There's no other way
Don't hug
Don't get too close now
Don't try and avoid it
It's the law now
You can't do this

You can't do that
I don't care if you're crying
I'm keeping you trapped
Stay safe
Inside
This will end after a while
It didn't?
Oh well
Just a little bit longer
Be a little bit stronger
It's for a good cause
It really is
So, go on
In this mess
Let's all be nice
Stay at home
Protect the NHS
Save lives

Hope

Sophia Kunxu Dou

Hope is my glasses
I have mistaken it for my eyes

Until one day
I looked up into the sky

The storm rained upon it
The hail punched it

And until my life had it shattered away
Was I able to see the world
Clearly for the first time -

In pitch darkness
I only saw the darkness

I fall and I crawl
And searched upon the ground

And hope is the mud on my hands
But I mould it into light

One Night the World Changed

Rose Elstob

One night the world changed,
Instead of school,
A computer,
Instead of freedom,
Quarantine and lockdown,
Instead of a breath of air,
A mask obscuring half your face,
In one night, the world changed,

One night our world changed,
The warnings of wreckage,
Worst in the UK,
Roofs blown off,
Deserted schools,
All from one little storm,
In one night, our world changed,

Last night the world changed,
Who does it help invading Ukraine,
We thought we got past this,
Why can't we just live in peace,
None of us need a World War three,
Can't we just live a normal life?

Poppies

Kira Nicholas

As dawn breaks upon the broken battlefields,

As pretty poppies prosper on the remnants of war,

We remember the dreary, dismal memories of combat.

The raging roar of the stuttering guns

And the heavy-hearted, holy goodbyes,

With the depressing drawing-down of blinds

As smoking guns become the last excess of conflict,

Its smoke a ghost as it drifts away.

A soldier cascades to the ground,

As tear gas blasts briskly throughout the terrible trenches,

Soon filling it to the brim.

The restless recruits instantly fumble with their gas masks,

Sweating and shivering in an abundance of fear

Yet only the lucky, fortunate ones survive,

As many descend towards the grimy, grubby ground.

Tears fly from the remaining troopers,

Still reeling from the dreadful, disturbing event,

Their hearts beating like a rambunctious drum.

All the young soldiers trembled with jittery fear and anxiety,

As the horrendous hatred of the guns rang loudly in their ears.

The thoughts of being with their sympathetic, devoted families

Was the only comforting image in their troubled minds.

With new-found determination, they grabbed their protective guns,

Their leather boots squelched as they sank slowly onto the ground.

Trepidation swiftly overcame them as they ascended the rusty ladder,

No Man's Land was before them...

Timorous troopers surrender themselves fearfully

Trembling with terror to the speedy sputtering of the rapid rifles' roaring rattle,

And as it boisterously thunders across the abhorrent battlefield,

They fade away like shining, sparkling stars in the morning.

Losing their light to the stunning, shiny sun...

Pretty poppies prosper on the remnants of war,

And as their pleasant petals drift between the crosses,

We are silent and still.

We remember those who courageously enlisted to fight for our country,

Those who passed from this wonderous earth,

And those who still clutch the mortifying memories of fighting on the front line.

Their valiant victory rightfully lies at the heart of the national anthem.

Adult 16+ Poetry

Two Sides of the Same Ocean (Calais November 2021)

Jo Burridge

Dear little boy

Just like my son he stands, smiling.

All bundled up in his big winter coat

And a small rucksack on his back.

Just like my son, he stands expectant

Excited,

His eyes shining.

My son does this when we're at a railway station.

On the edge of a platform.

(I call him back, behind the yellow lines, to keep him safe and hold his hand.)

Both little boys are excited about the journey to come. Their new adventures.

Just like my son, this dear little boy has been told of the things he'll be able to see and do. Taste and hear.

Even though it's cold, he is snug in his coat. And so excited he probably doesn't notice the cold. Little ones often don't. Their parents keep them safe and warm.

He smiles for the camera and gives a cheeky thumbs up sign.

It's nearly time for his exciting journey.

Just like my son, his mother holds his hand. She tells him of the adventures ahead and how she'll keep him safe.

But then, not like my son,

He waits by the water's edge.

There is no line to keep safe behind.

This dear little boy stands on the wrong side of the same sea.

His parents can't protect him.

There are no guarantees.

The hope for a place of safety propels them on through treacherous seas.

By accident, not design, he stands there and my son stands here.

Random chance places each little boy on his side of the sea.

They Changed the Timetable

Shaun McDonald

The trials of life apply to all
poets too are forced to wait.
Timetables, blight of great and small,
chaos when the bus is late.

T S Elliot lost in Wasteland,
lost from light of the sun.
Wasting and waiting in blood and sand
all because the bus didn't run.

Betjeman tried to flee from Slough
before bombs began to fall.
He trembled alone, didn't know how
to escape, when no buses at all.

Dylan Thomas did not Go Lightly
to the funeral of his Dad.
Buses meant to run twice nightly
timetable wrong and the service was bad.

Masefield never made it to the sea again,
the lonely sea and the sky.
Bus service shut down in heavy rain,
no star to steer him by.

In Xanadu did Kubla Khan,
an epic verse cut back by fate.
The irritating Porlock man
asking why the bus was late.

Poet laureate lost the role
of rhyming for the Queen.
Missed her birthday, left her cold;
they cancelled the No.17

And so it is, our peace depends
on reason and the dance of rhyme.
On bright beginnings and right ends,
so long as buses run on time.

Snow

John Blackmore

I've had dreams rent by summer thunder
As it prowls round the night-shrouded hills
With growls spilling over the pregnant pauses,
Shot through with lightning
That rattles the stifling air I breathe.

I've known nights where sleep is plundered
By frenzied gusts bending squall-splattered windows,
Like ships' sails underway,
While I lie still:
Defiantly calm in the face of the marauding wind
That scatters plant pots and blasts patio chairs into disarray.

But the weather that always catches me unawares
Is the silent snow that falls
Soft and insidious in the dark.
Back-lit curtains rouse me from my slumbers,
With the ethereal ice-blue glow
Of a new world, bright and soundless.

It's Been Ten Years Now

Valerie-Jane Morley

Black curly hair
With your model good looks
But you did smoke.
The gifts, the flowers
Then a roast dinner
Your signature dish.

Tennis in the garden
You sun-tanned in one day.
Summers with the girls in play -
Cold tea in saucers.
Memories. Insects in amber now.

Your very scent
Ripe grapes and hockey kit.
You come, you go - that inner tidal flow I wrap up, keep
safe.
The brave, strong and the true of you.

A Grip on Life

Sally Green

New to the world
Strong presence
Tiny wrinkled hands
Tight grip

Small person now
School-run
Hand in hand
Tight grip

Exploring, challenging youth
Walks alone
Hands on mobile
Tight grip

Gangly long limbs
Teenage love
Hands long for
Tight grip

Grown in stature
Welcoming smile
Hand stretched out
Tight grip

Passion and promises
True Love
Hands entwined
Tight grip

Their new life
Strong presence
Tiny wrinkled hands
Tight grip

Bordeaux

Macaque

In a village on the Garonne,
Forty summers ago, I watched
With shy fascination –

>Just a boy
>Ending a vacation
>Breaking a long journey home.

I stood in the stone square
And watched her pressing
Grapes in a large wooden tub –

>Just a peasant girl
>Treading the grapes
>As her mother and grandmother had done.

I watched her, skirt folded to thigh,
Hair tied in a scarf, her simple blouse
Swelling before her like a sail as she worked.

I watched her feline movements,
Her legs glistening to the knee,
Bare feet splitting the skins of the grapes,
The heady juice pouring from a spout in the tub.

I watched the dark ringlet that danced
At her temple, her dark eyes under the bright sun,
Freckled cheeks, up-turned nose, her lips
As they burst like a grape
Releasing her intoxicating smile.

Just the memory of a child.

But, with every glass of wine
I see her face, her smile,
I see her bare legs, sticky and sweet –

I raise my glass
And kiss her feet.

Stalker with a small 's'

Esme Hayes

Collectors, benign—

Your humble grandad assembling model cars

Your kinder egg-consuming child,

Your gig mementoes in a drawer

Is my address written on the body of the cars?

Is my address in the instructions in the capsule?

Does the order of the tour dates on the band t-shirt spell out my

address?

Customers, benign—

Someone asking for avocados, again

Man crouching to stare at the reductions bay

Walking the old man's bags to his car

Are they vengeful about the non-appearance of fresh bread, or garlic bulbs, or the display blocking wheelchair access?

Was he staring at the reductions as a foil to catch glances of me?

Did he feign frailty to get me to touch his things, to get closer to me?

Managers, benign—
Asking me to come in outside of schedule
Breaking the law
Cracking unfortunate jokes

Should I have sucked up to him?
Should I have toed the line?
Would he have ever done anything to stop it?

Love interests, benign—
Going for a walk,
What films do you watch oh I watch these films have you
watched those films,
Sex,

Should I have pushed them harder?
Should I have hit him?
Were they always like that?

Strangers, benign—
People feeding birds,
A woman talks to me about the dying beech trees,
A man on the train was a counsellor

Why do you know my address?
Where did you get my address?
How did you find my address?

Laundrette owners, benign—
Can I have £5 in change please?
Can I leave it in the machine, I'll be back in ten minutes
Thank you, Thank you

Can I have £5 in change please?
Can I leave it in the machine, I'll be back in ten minutes
Thank you, Thank you
Please can I keep my dog with me
I have him with me now since I got stalked
Yes, yes of course. I'll take him back to the car now

People, benign—
How are you?
Come in!
What do you do these days?

You, benign—
Following me
Sending things to my address

A stranger
Oh. Are you sure?
What if they just really like you?
They're probably just a very nervous person

A person
A customer
A stranger

A collector
A manager
A love interest

Watching me
Tracking me

A stranger
A person
A person

A grandad
A stranger
A stranger
A stranger
A stranger

This poem appears in an altered form to suit the
publication format.

Low Lighthouse

Ash Dean

Looking alive for a life,

Stepping out

As if the tide wandered further than she liked –

Low Lighthouse, *en pointe*,

Accentuates the arc that's flushed in the flats

Striped and saturated, a running track bend

For whippets, humans and sand gnats

Homing in on this beacon,

The icon of the plain,

Whose nine worthies together

Raise her body aloft come sun, wind or rain,

A figure benevolent, modest and pure

Making vivid her maternal ribbon

To see us born from the river to the sea

Safe from the traps of her shore.

Short Stories

Under 11 Short Stories

The Dragon Ruins

Joseph Williams

It was a turbulent night as the troop of lightning bolts descended on the grimy ground. A flock of grey, moist clouds soared in unison over the gleaming temple that proudly perched on a colossal, jagged mountain. In front of the worn birch door sat a small, brown-haired boy with a metallic sword laid down by his side. The boy was called Logan and the ruin he stood on right now used to be a luscious civilisation where plants spurted from the simplest of gardens and thrived with glee. Now corrupted, a temple was built, a piece of protection for a dragon!

Logan grabbed his sword and threw it at the golden padlock which locked it and BAM!, the door opened! He slowly trekked into the ancient temple, his blade grasped in his muddy hand, but when he was about to walk in, three bulky gargoyles ripped themselves free of their drenched stands! The names carved in the stands crumbled to dust as they fluttered around in the blue sky.

The smallest gargoyle skimmed towards Logan but he was running closer and closer to the temple's left wall. When he was only about 10cm from the wall, he leapt backwards as the gargoyle crashed into the temple, leaving a child-sized hole. Its pieces were suddenly transported into a chained-up room, as Logan front-flipped into the hole and grabbed a crossbow that was lying on the gold and white patch-work carpet.

He violently pulled the string with the arrow and let go, then the arrow swiftly flew right into the second gargoyle, knocking him out cold. Though Logan had eliminated the first two with ease, the third gargoyle flew in the door and grabbed him! It threw him down a man-hole but Logan somehow got pushed up and landed in a dirty dim-lit dungeon with his enemy, the dragon, in front of him.

It was a crimson red beast with golden horns and undulating wings the size of a skyscraper! Then Logan stabbed the creature. Its roar louder than a siren and it blew fire out of its sticky mouth. Logan was scarred but he knew what to do. He ran to the tail, dodging fireballs, and ran up onto it to destroy him, he hit the dragon's back. The dragon crumbled to dust, as a dark gem formed and Logan smashed it! The land was green again and everyone was healed, even Logan's scar faded! The world was safe again! The end!

Different and Loved

Gracie Llewellyn

Once upon a time there was a family of rainbow coloured hearts. There was a Blue heart in the family. He was sad because he was the only one who was blue and he was different to his family.

One day the Blue heart went for a walk in the dark, shadowy woods because he was sad. He saw a happy Red heart, who said "I am different from my family."

The Blue heart said "I am different from my family too, but why are you so happy?"

The Red heart said "Because I know that my family loves me."

The Blue heart went back to his family and said "I'm home" and the family said "We thought we lost you and we love you."

The Blue heart was happy again because he knew his family loved him.

The Blue heart ran to find the Red heart to thank her for helping him to know that his family loves him too.

The Blue heart now knows it's ok to be different.

Fen the Super Pig!

Mackenzie Morris

Fen is a normal pig who is being held captive by an evil Wizard called Leo.

Leo can't cast spells, his magic only allows him to create potions. He was going to test his potions on test subjects, aka animals, and Fen was one of his subjects. Fen has been captive since he was a piglet, and he is not happy about that!

Leo is creating a potion that allows him to fly and shoot lasers from his eyes. The potion smells nasty so he injects it into an apple. He has to cook the apple, so he puts it in the oven and starts cleaning a shelf.

Leo doesn't notice that he's accidentally knocked a bottle of wine off the shelf which falls on top of the oven door. The door pops open and the apple rolls into Fen's cage. Fen is starving and he loves apples, so he eats it!

He starts to glow vibrant orange, shake and his eyes uncontrollably blast lasers which cut through the cage door. Fen sees his chance to escape. He makes a run for it whilst Leo isn't looking and goes outside. He sees that he's been living in a dark grey magical tower on top of a dome that can only be seen when the door is open. He sees a farm in the distance and runs towards it.

Leo realizes the oven door is open and sees that the apple has disappeared. Then he sees that Fen's cage door is broken and Fen has vanished as well. Mmm maybe I shouldn't have added laser eyes to the potion mix he thinks! ARRGH WHERE IS FEN. He realizes the pig has eaten the apple which had his magic potion in!

He's furious and chases after Fen screaming 'I'll turn

you into pork chops!'

Fen is scared that Leo will catch and eat him. He runs very quickly and then his trotters are no longer on the ground, he's flying!

Fen looks down and thinks arrgh stop following me. Fen thinks maybe I can trap him in a pit. He fires his laser eyes at the ground and creates a deep hole.

Leo is so busy looking up at the flying pig he doesn't see the trap, trips over a rock and falls into it. He lands at the bottom and realizes he surrounded by lava and there is no way out.

Leo shouts 'help me'! Fen feels happy that he's escaped but feels a bit guilty that Leo is now stuck in lava! He thinks maybe if I save him, he'll be nice and change his ways.

Fen flies into the pit and saves Leo.

Now that Leo is out of the pit, Fen asks for permission to set all the other animals free. Leo agrees and says sorry, promising to be a kind wizard from now on.

Fen realizes he's now a Super Pig and is very happy!

The World Under Your Toaster

Mia Shore

Have you ever thought of anything living under the toaster? If you don't think there is anything living there this story will prove you wrong. A long time ago there was a scientist family. They did lots of crazy stuff which made the house go wild. One day a size experiment went really, really wrong. It made the family go…teeny tiny! So tiny, even smaller than the point of a pen! At first, they didn't know where they were but then they saw they were right by the toaster. They looked under it and the child saw something move! This is where the story begins!

At first the thing looked like a toast crumb but then it revealed to be a person carrying a toast crumb! As they looked around, they realised there was a colossal village…under the toaster! The scientist family started to explore. The people were the same as them and they did the same things. They were also scientists! The toaster people welcomed the new family and showed them around. They saw a red swimming pool made of…jam and lots of other crazy things such as houses made of crumbs! After a while the scientists were getting hungry.

"Don't worry," said the toaster people "the scientists always put toast on!"

"Hang on…we're the scientists!!"

"Oh no!"

"Don't worry there's plenty of crumbs to keep us going.

After they finally got eating, they were showed to their rooms in a crumb hotel where everything was made of crumbs stuck with jam or marmite! They had a good night, but they kept waking up because the bed was hard, bumpy and lumpy! They were tired but said they were ready for making and experimenting. They were a little worried that they only had breadcrumbs, butter splodges, jam, honey and marmite to use but they worked hard and managed to make a time machine…with a little help from the plug socket!

"Don't go yet," said the crumb people. "We need some help with the monster that lives under the microwave!"

"Look, we have to go but when we are big again we will clean under the microwave for you and get rid of the monster!"

So, the scientists climbed in their crumb time machine and said goodbye. But what nobody realised was that when you go back in time your memory goes back in time as well and you forget everything! So, when they returned they wondered what had happened but were tired and went to bed. The next morning they decided to carry out a size experiment but it went really, really wrong! And they ended up…you guessed it…under the toaster again!

Have you ever wondered what lives under your toaster?! Maybe you should go and have a look now! You may be surprised!

The Shooting Star

Evellyn Farnham

One day a little girl called Ruby was playing in the garden and saw a star, but it wasn't an ordinary star, it was a star that was moving – it was gold and silver and sparkled as it whizzed through the night sky. What was it she said out loud to herself? She thought it could be aliens coming to Earth, do they really exist? Ruby ran inside to find her mum, if Aliens were about to land, they needed to warn people.

Ruby's mum was washing the dishes when Ruby came bursting in through the kitchen door. 'Quick, quick aliens are about to land', said Ruby – they must have come all the way from planet Zong. Ruby's mum hadn't taken much notice of Ruby's excitable entrance into the room, Ruby often had an imagination that was fit for a fairy tale. 'There are no such things as Alien's', said Ruby's mum, 'it must have been a shooting star, did you make wish?'.

'NO', said Ruby, 'I didn't make a wish, but I wish I could meet an alien from planet Zong'.

Ruby went to bed that night thinking about the shooting star that she had seen. At school she had been learning all about space; so Ruby knew that the bright flash of light falling through the night sky was an object entering the Earth's protective layer – it was a little bit like a suit of armour, except the Earth's armour was so hot that when anything came through, it turned into a big hot ball of fire.

Ruby fell fast asleep thinking about meeting an Alien. Then Ruby heard a strange beeping noise coming from underneath her bed! Ruby jumped up and listened – the noise came again. Ruby needed to investigate; she leant over the edge of her bed and slowly lifted the quilt cover.

There in the middle of the floor, underneath Ruby's bed, was an Alien in the shape of a star - it looked very sad. Ruby reached out to grab the star, but it was too hot to touch. Ruby asked the star why he looked so sad. The star said, my sister fell from the sky and I can't find her. I think I might know where she is said Ruby and she asked the star to follow her into the garden.

There in the corner of the garden, glowing faintly in a dark hole, was the star that Ruby had seen falling from the sky. The alien star was amazed and started to get brighter – it was feeling happy again. The alien star jumped into the hole and together they both started to climb up into the night sky. Suddenly there was a burst of light and both stars shot into the sky and disappeared.

Ruby woke up with a fright – she had been dreaming! Shooting stars were Aliens and she had seen one. She couldn't wait to tell her mum in the morning that wishes do come true.

11 to 15 Short Stories

Scarlett War

Kitty McAlonan

William's cheeks burnt up into a deep red colour, his forehead damp with sweat and his feeble, weak legs shook vigorously. He lay in a creaky, old, oak bed in a dark room. The room was small and bare- its ceilings were off-white, and the floors were made of wood that squeaked if any weight was put upon them. The room had a slightly musty aroma, which surrounded them strongly. Rosanna, his older sister, bent over him and placed a wet towel on his head. A tear filled up in her eye as she stared into the face of her brother who had been so badly hurt by Scarlett Fever. She caressed her hands through his mousy brown hair and left the room.

"Father, what will I do? We need him to evacuate soon. Here and Glasgow is supposed to be the most dangerous place he can be."

"Calm down Rosanna," George, their father, replied in a soft tone. "You both will leave London tomorrow morning, early. You will both get on the first train leaving to the Southwest. You will both live there for however long it needs to be until it's safe for you to return. And you my daughter, will take care of my son."

"But," Rosanna tried to reply.

"Not another word about it. I have to leave tonight for the war," George interrupted in a dismissive tone and turned down the barely lit hall.

Rosanna was nervous. How could she get her William onto the train? She lay down next to her sick brother on the cold floor. Rosanna thought to herself, "There's no way William will be allowed on! But I don't want him to die without me!" A singular tear rolled down Rosanna's freckled skin and her deep emerald eyes filled up.

The next day she woke William up his temperature so high his head felt as if it was burning. William pushed up his frail body till he sat up straight.

"Will, we need to leave today. It's not safe for us to be here anymore. Father has to stay though but I'll be with you the whole time," Rosanna soothed William. He opened his mouth to speak but his throat was too sore to even make a little peep. He nodded. His broken eyes looked worried though- drained of any happiness- creased from the pain.

Rosanna went downstairs to find a note left by their father,

"I left late last night my children. You will have to wear these tags when on the train- join the rest of William's old school year and enjoy your time down in Cornwall. I will see you soon, Father." Rosanna's hands shook slightly as she read the note. She took a deep breath and packed up all her belongings into a little luggage bag.

Rosanna walked William to the train station an hour later- his body practically hanging on hers. She clambered through the station packed with distraught parents hugging their children. Young girls and boys hurried onto the big train each with their favourite teddies and a bag full of clothes. A little tag was pinned onto each child- their ticket to safety. Rosanna buried her arm around William's mouth- practically suffocating him, however, she knew she needed to protect anyone from catching his disease.

"Hollow Hill" William's primary school he attended before he got sick. Rosanna rushed over to the sign and gathered with the school's guardians. After taking a register the group walked onto their area of the train. Rosanna waited towards the back and just as soon as everyone was out of sight, she carried William and ran quickly to the back of the train. At the end, there was a little door with a sign "Do not open. Workers only." Rosanna panicked slightly and put William down. She knew that through this door she could sit on the ledge outside to keep William from infecting anyone. She also knew she should not go out there. She also knew she was going to open that door. She checked to see if anyone was watching and pushed down on the handle. It was locked. What could she do now? Suddenly a train attendee started walking towards her. She grabbed William and quickly looked around. "Lavatory" In big, bold writing shone to the left of their heads. She opened the door and chucked Will's frail body, rather forcefully, inside.

"What's going on here?" The bulky attendee asked.

"Oh," Rosanna said thinking on her feet, "My brother was desperate to use the lavatory. I said I would wait outside for him as he doesn't want to be by himself."

"Well, you two better get back to your guardians straight away after, you need to stay in your groups," He replied unsympathetically and stumbled back up the hallway into the next carriage. A sigh of relief overcame her once he was gone. Rosanna unclipped a pin in her hair and straightened it out. She inserted it into the lock and after a minute of fiddling, she managed to unlock the door to the outside. She pulled William back out from the lavatory and with a final glance of the surroundings, she vigorously pushed open the door and clambered out with her brother. She lay her brother down onto the little ledge at the end of the train and pulled out some clothes and blankets from her bag to give him comfort. She sat by his side the whole six-hour journey filled with pride knowing she kept him safe.

A couple of months later

Rosanna sat by William's side yet again however this time he sat up next to her as well. They were on a small beach enclosed by precipitous cliffs that looked down over them. To the right of them was an old lady who very kindly took them in.

"We're safe now," Rosanna thought and with those words, she closed her eyes and lay on the soft sand.

Pink Shrimp

Matilda Taylor

One scorching day - in 2050 – a young, unbothered boy (Matthew aged 12) arrived at a zoo called "Greg's Zoo". His serene parents raced off, leaving the boy covered in desert dust. Matthew looked at the disorganized zoo that did not have even an ounce of sound or anyone in sight. It looked as if it was abandoned.

"Matthew, Matthew my boy, welcome, welcome to the wonderful zoo full of joy!" Uncle Greg chirped.

Matthew whispered under his breath, 'more like full of depression.' "Hi Uncle Greg…" Matthew spoke softly as the high-spirited man smacked the poor boy's shoulder leaving a mark as red as a tomato.

Uncle Greg opened his arms, with his back towards Matthew, as he entered the unkempt zoo abounding in dismay. Unfortunately, not a human in sight decided to even walk near the zoo; it was clear to say that Greg had an unsuccessful way of entertaining others – even his own nephew.

"Why is this place so dull?" Matthew questioned forgetting that some things that are said are meant to be kept in the mind; not said out-loud.

"Well, business has been bad lately, however, I do have high hopes. In fact, I think you can come and help me, come feed the animals with me, I'm sure the lion will appreciate your kindness." Greg announced with a booming voice just as he pulled the sore arm of Matthew and heaved him to the lion's cage. Frozen dead, Matthew stood there wrapping his arms around his body trying to force warmth with his fast, up, and down motion.

"Hold this my boy, today it's your chance to experience some work" Greg spat. Throwing buckets of smelly meat to the mouth-watering, lip-licking, open-eyed child. Greg slobbered his way to where the vulnerable lion laid, licking its paw, and seeking its eyes on the scared boy as if he was ready to pounce high. As quick as lightning, the beast threw the pieces of meat down his throat, polishing every speck of it.

"Do the lions only eat meat?" Matthew muttered as Greg laughed out a short speech (he could eat you). Matthew rose to his uncle's attention, for a second, he was left with a petrified look until he realised, he was joking.

"No, other greasy food but I don't have that kind of money, same with other animals, they only have one food they eat."

"Like what?" Matthew asked summoning a cheeky plan.

"The rhinos eat leaves, monkeys eat bananas, flamingos eat shrimp…"

"Wait flamingos eat shrimp?"

"Yes, how else do you think they are pink?"

Matthew looks around the empty zoo and has an idea….

"Hey, Uncle Greg do you think I can feed the rest of the animals."

"Sure, I guess, I do have some bills to pay." Greg whimpered as he walked away with his tears nearly running down his face. Matthew ran off, which was the only sort of excitement surrounding the stranded zoo, grabbing the shrimp, and forcing himself to pick the blush-coloured, squishy animals up and providing it to the lion.

Guzzling them down one by one, the lion looked at the energized child that had an excited smile extending his face in the broken, artificial light.

Matthew wanted to feed the lion shrimp to see if the monstrous animal would turn pink just like how flamingos turn rouge with their rosy food! For days, Matthew was left to feed all the animals, still, the only one he took pride on was the lion that was getting pinker every day.

"Matthew, my boy, my main man, how are my animals…going" Greg said with an open-mouthed jaw, coming round the corner of the lion cage. "MATTHEW WHY IS MY LION PINK?!" Greg shouted as his face was engulfed with rage.

"I, I fed the lion shrimp to make him pink, please don't get mad at me." Matthew begged, pleaded.

"MAD, I'M NOT MAD, I'M FURI…" Greg stuttered as he witnessed an innocent woman walking up and admiring the pink lion.

"Sorry to disturb you guys, this is an amazing creature, it's glowing in pink glory. Sorry, I'm Natalie, the head of 'Animal Agent' the new animal newspaper, I need to document this!" Natalie smiled as she got out an as-it-seemed important pen and a stack of crisp white paper.

"Of course, Matthew a word…this is amazing thank you, hey what about feeding all the animals' shrimp, we can have a pink zoo, I'll finally make some money." Greg smiled, overjoyed with the happenings his nephew performed, whilst he slid smoothly over to the journalist, who grinned and disappeared silently – the zoo was once again quiet, but only for a small amount of time.

The next day, when Greg opened the doors, there were floods of bustling people crowded around, intrigued to even get a glimpse of the majestic animal. Excitedly, Greg let in all the people only to realise the queue carried on for hours (the cash register even overflowed from all the money he was making).

"How's the other pink money-making animals going Matthew?" Greg shouted in exhilaration as Matthew explained it would take around a week to form the gleeful man's wishes. "Can't wait!"

Over time, only pink animals could be seen at the now-called 'Pink Zoo', and it was all because of Matthew's wacky idea that led to not only, a happy uncle; healthier animals, better zoo but as well as an entertainment company that millions of people came to from all over the world. Intriguingly, Matthew found a passion in life and made amazing discoveries of rainbow-coloured, enthusiastic animals that became the world's biggest shock.

The Cosy Cafe on the Corner of Town

Sasha Keates

In a rather grand living room a woman sat with her two children, she was preparing to recite a tale of happiness and heartbreak, and the story went like this:

Lonely in a cosy cafe on the corner of town, a woman who lived without hope sat unaware that she was about to meet her soulmate. Walking along the snowy street was an optimistic man, praying that somewhere would be open despite the heavy snow storm falling from the sky - and it was. The cosy cafe on the corner of the street was open.

It was a tiny place that wasn't exactly well known - the cafe was popular to those who knew it was there, but a random stranger walking past wouldn't be aware. Inside were comfy sofas and many cushioned chairs. There was a tiny library, a few paintings and a small serving bar tucked away in the corner. It was a happy place; one that put a smile on others' faces even if their day had been unkind.

Life had drowned the woman many times and she had given up. It was funny that a woman who didn't show much emotion worked as a waitress in a cafe full of joy. She sat by herself cuddled up with a blanket, reading a book filled with poems. When a bell rang. It was a signal - telling the workers that a new customer had entered the cafe, and was ready to be served. In walked the man from before, his wide smile was contagious and filled others with happiness. The man walked up to the bar grinning at the woman. They say when you meet the love of your life, time stops. Everyone and everything went silent as the man walked towards the woman. He seemed to pace in slow motion. Time had in fact frozen.

"What can I get you?"

"Surprise me,"

And with an impatient eye roll she moved to get started with the drink. The conversation that followed was short and sweet, a few jokes were made in an attempt to make the woman smile. A few genuine laughs had managed to escape the cage she had locked them in. She was happy.

"I know your trick, I said surprise me so you chose the most expensive thing on the menu."

The reply was a small smile, and a slightly confused look in her eyes, as she wondered how the man had figured it out. Perhaps she had underestimated him.

Their connection was like a magnet. They were two opposites, but were still attracted to one another. Their connection was powerful and strong, they just didn't know it yet. And she wouldn't realise it until it was too late.

Fast forward a couple of years, and the two strangers had progressed to much more. He had taught her how to love. She had taught him that life wasn't always perfect. He had inspired her to try new things. She had supported him.

The season was now summer, the sun blasted its rays down to the tortured ground. Most melted in the extreme temperatures, and the cosy cafe was busier than ever - as it was one of the only buildings with air conditioning.

Inside, the woman was trapped making endless amounts of ice cold drinks. Every new customer was more miserable than the previous, she struggled to keep her patience, but a gentle reminder was by her side, persuading her to carry on.

"You know, it's gotten to the point where you might as well work here alongside me."

"I thought about it for a second, but I much prefer sitting here watching you attempt to be nice to every customer."

"It's suffocating me!"

"Relax, you only have a couple more hours,"

"Yeah! And the weather is supposed to be getting warmer."

A shared laughter filled the warm air as the woman dragged another bag of ice out of the freezer.

"I better be off I have that appointment to get to,"

The two embraced and said their goodbyes and she watched as the man left, a feeling in her stomach was warning her of what was to come, but she didn't listen. She simply got back to work and carried on ignoring the impatient customers snapping their fingers in the poor girl's face.

After the appointment, the man walked back into the cafe, but something about him was different, he was in pain. A look of terror and innocence overwhelmed his eyes. These emotions were soon reflected in the woman's.

"I have cancer."

His final months were spent well, they were full of passion, full of happiness, full of adventure. And when it came to the man's last moments, despite being in absolute agony, he still managed to remain optimistic:

"Don't cry, life has treated me well."

A startled look appeared on the woman's face,

"How on earth can you say that after all the suffering it's caused you?"

"I met you and I was happy. I want you to promise me that when I'm gone you will continue to love to the fullest"

"Why?"

"Because life isn't worth living unless there is love."

Her vision was blurred due to the tsunami of tears that had been forced to stay put. Those were his final words. After that, he went silent.

Back to the family in the living room. The mother sat in her chair

trembling and the children looked equally as devastated.

"The man in the story - the one who was happy, he was our father wasn't he?"

The woman gave a simple nod as a timid smile appeared on her face.

"And the woman, that's you."

"I promised him I would fill my life with love, and I did, I cherish and love him, and the two of you."

She looked out of the window overlooking a busy street, then she looked up into the peaceful night sky and gazed at the stars, knowing that one of them was him.

Beyond Tristan

Alex Shaw-Young

Simon stood staring, trying desperately to block the thoughts that rushed around his mind like a million different fireflies fighting for his attention. His eyes barely registered his surroundings. The grass blowing gently in the early winter wind. The cold stone walls of the church looming above him. The bell knelled for the eleventh hour, breaking through his mental barricade and taking him to a time he would never forget.

*****

Tristan sighed next to him as they sat together on the overgrown church wall overlooking the town below them.

"What is it?" Simon asked.

"There's something you should know," Tristan said, avoiding Simon's eyes.

"You can tell me anything," he said gently.

Tristan nodded and sighed again, staring into the distance. "I've been, I've been diagnosed with cancer. The doctors say I could have had it for as long as a year."

Simon tried desperately to keep control of his emotions, Tristan had enough to deal with, without putting more pressure on him. "That's honestly, really crap."

Tristan smiled sadly, "Yeah it is." He turned to Simon as tears began to roll down his cheeks. "You know, I never thought that..." he broke off.

"I'm always here for you. You know that." Simon hugged him closely as tear after tear fell down Tristan's cheeks. They stayed like that for a long time, the silence that spoke more than words ever could.

*****

That had been the moment his life had begun to change forever. Another memory pushed to the surface, dragging him to another place and time that he remembered all too well.

*****

It was three months later that Simon walked into Tristan's bedroom which was covered in posters of his favourite bands. A picture pinned to the wall of the two of them smiling at the viewer with the church tall and dark in the background was a stark reminder of happier times. Tristan lay in his bed on the far side of his room opposite the PlayStation that rested on his desk. His eyes were closed as he slept, exhaustion painted plainly across his pale face. Quietly, Simon tucked the duvet around him and crept back towards the open bedroom door.

"Wait," Tristan's voice called, his voice weak and tired. Simon turned to see him struggling to sit up in his bed. "Please sit with me a bit, I need a bit of normal."

Simon slowly sat on the bed, the springs creaking beneath his weight. "I got your message. How was it?"

"A little uncomfortable, as you might imagine if someone was to stuff a drugged needle into the vein of your arm," Tristan said, slightly irritably. He gestured at the white plaster taped neatly against his translucent skin.

Simon scrunched his nose, "What did the doctor say?"

"Simon, I need a little bit of normal in this crazy world at the moment. I get interrogated enough by an endless supply of nurses and doctors who ask the same questions over and over again. It gets a little tiring when people are always asking you how you're feeling all the time," Tristan paused then continued, "I'm sorry, it's just-"

"It's fine, I get it. I'd be the same," Simon interrupted softly.

"You want to play Call of Duty?" Tristan asked, breaking the awkward silence that engulfed the room.

"Sure," Simon smiled and moved to switch on the PlayStation.

*****

Simon tried to stop the tears that threatened to take hold as he walked amongst the gravestones that stood silently like a platoon of merciless soldiers. The chemotherapy hadn't worked as the doctors had hoped and Tristan's condition had deteriorated, his energy drained easily even in the simplest of activities. Eventually, he was moved to hospital as the doctors monitored and did everything they could. Another memory surfaced and he surrendered to it as it pulled him down to its darkest depths.

*****

The hospital curtains were open as Simon walked in. Tristan was asleep on the hospital bed, barely visible, surrounded by tubes and monitors beeping incessantly. Tristan's mum Jo slumped in the corner of the room. She looked like she hadn't slept in weeks, dark circles drooping down her face.

"Hello Simon," she whispered. "He's asleep at the moment."

Simon nodded slowly, swallowing hard at the sight of Tristan.

"Please sit," Jo said quietly her eyes teary. "There's something I've got to tell you."

Simon felt like he had no control over his own body as he slowly sank onto the chair beside Tristan.

"I just spoke with the doctor; the scans came back and," Jo paused and swallowed before continuing. Deep down he knew what was coming but he didn't want to believe it. "There's nothing they can do to help him. They said the cancer has spread too much and he doesn't have much time left. My poor baby boy," Jo sobbed into her hands.

It hit him like a knife in the back. He'd left soon after not waiting for Tristan to wake. He couldn't stay any longer, not with the knowledge that one day he'd wake up to a world without Tristan in it. He wasn't strong enough to face him, not today.

It was less than two weeks later, that he woke up to the sound of rain pattering at his window for the first time in weeks. He found his phone with a message from Jo saying that Tristan had passed away in the night. There were three missed calls from him and a voice message. Tears fell, streaming freely down his cheeks as his whole body shook with sobs.

*****

That had been almost six months ago, he still hadn't managed to find the courage to open the voice message. It was time. Simon stared at the gravestone with the name Tristan Myers permanently etched into its face. Daffodils swayed lightly as Simon, with tears rolling down his cheeks, finally pressed play. Tristan's voice spoke gently out of the phone's microphone as the church's clock struck twelve.

Gift

Ivy Silver

She died on Monday, but I didn't know until Thursday. We were supposed to go ice-skating that weekend and my mum wanted to know what time to drop me off. Nobody answered when she phoned in the morning, but it was only 7:55 after all.

I knew something was wrong the moment I got home. My call of "I'm back!" was answered with silence before I heard my mum's all too quiet voice telling me to come to the dining room.

"Abby's dad called," my she began, "sweetie, there was an accident…" They went on to explain everything with timid voices and hands on my shoulders. How Abby had been walking to her grandma's just like she did every Monday, how it had been raining hard and the driver hadn't seen her in time.

I remember everything about that day until then so clearly, but after that, my memories are blurred. Cold cups of tea, the view from my bedroom window, people telling me they were here if I needed anything. The funeral was filled with strangers. I sat near the back and listened to stories I'd heard before because she'd told me herself. I wanted to share my own: about the girl wearing rainbow socks I'd met at the bus stop after missing both our busses; about exchanging numbers; about one hangout turning into two and then three, until we were seeing each other almost every week. I wanted to talk about lying on Abby's bed and telling her she was my favourite person in the world. She had turned to face me and smiled. "You're my favourite person too."

I stayed home for as long as I could but in the end, I

found myself back in a class full of people who had never met Abby. For the first few weeks, my friends talked softly around me, and the teachers asked how I was doing, but after a while people started to believe me when I said that I was fine, and my world went back to normal. I wasn't fine. I did my work, played netball, and talked to people when I had to, but I was nowhere near fine. I cried the most the eighth week after the accident, and at 2:53am, sixty-one days since Abby had died, something in me snapped. I pulled on boots and a cardigan and crept outside, shutting the front door softly behind me.

I'd watched enough movies about grief to know that I was doing it wrong. I wished I had a car to drive off into the night, or the money to buy a plane ticket to somewhere we'd always dreamt of going. Instead, I ran. The wind whipped at my hair, the night air was freezing on my face, and I felt like I was flying. My feet thudded against the pavement without direction. The streetlights blurred around me. Everything was crumbling. The world that felt so wrong without Abby fell away. I wasn't part of it, and if Abby wasn't either then that must mean we were together again. Just me, her and the stars, just like all those times before. I wanted to go on running forever. This was where I belonged. I was happy. I closed my eyes and wished…

My eyes flew open as an engine roared in my ears, far too loud. A pair of blinding headlights hurtled towards me and swerved out of my line of vision. I heard the screech of tyres on tarmac and felt my body fly through the air, hitting the ground suddenly and rolling. It all happened so fast that it was only when I lay on my back, panting, that I realised I had just avoided being hit. My head was spinning and through my blurred vision I could make out a man running towards me. "Are you okay?" he shouted. "Miss are you okay?" I sat up, everything coming back into focus and the shock already beginning to wear off. "Yeah, I am."

The sun was just starting to peek red over the horizon as I walked slowly back home. I had scraped both my knees and there was a small cut on my left hand but apart from that I was fine. Still, the scene kept playing over and over in my head. The car had come so close. If the driver hadn't swerved in time, if I hadn't dived out of the way, then just like that I would be dead. Just like Abby was. What then? I thought about how lost I had been feeling since the accident. If it had been me, how would my parents cope? What about my friends I had been pushing away?

That morning over breakfast, I asked my parents about getting grief counselling. I texted all my friends, asking them to hang out. After some thought, I decided to reach out to a few of Abby's too. I messaged them over Instagram, introducing myself and asking if they wanted to talk sometime. If any of them were feeling like I had, I wanted to be there.

Afterwards, I walked down to the bus stop. There, I sat down and pulled out my phone to send one last text.

Abby, I remember you telling me once that life is a gift. It was stupid and clichéd, and I was crying over a maths test, but you were right. You also said that we only appreciate things once we have to live without them. To be fair, that was after you had lost your favourite pen but it's still true. Your life was a gift, and I think mine is too. I'm glad I didn't lose it last night. I really miss you and it's hard, but I have to do something with my gift of being alive, so I'm going to live. I promise.

Adult 16+ Short Stories

Girl of Your Fancy

Kevin Hayman

The inspector entered the small interview room and slid a cup across the coffee-stained table. 'Black, no sugar, wasn't it?'

'Thanks.' Ford was studying the room. 'This where the interrogations happen?'

'Not exactly.' The inspector took a seat opposite. He was good-looking for his age, rugged, with short greying hair and a muscular body that might once have been desirable to the women who appraised it. 'We use this room for more informal chats.'

'So, we won't need that?' Ford nodded to the double-deck tape machine.

'Well, you called the meeting; you tell me?'

'It might save me repeating myself.'

'Okay.' The inspector punched buttons on the machine. 'For the recording,' he said, 'this is Inspector Rothstein interviewing Cameron Ford at his request. It's Monday the 7th of March. 11:45 A.M.' He raised his eyebrows at Ford.

'I start now?'

'Yes.'

'Okay,' Ford said. 'Where to start?'

'Why not from the beginning?'

'That would mean going back a couple years.'

'I'm in no rush.'

'I remember the day, because I was watching football on TV, with my friend Craig. It was just after Christmas...

we were trying some speciality beers.'

The inspector nodded. 'Right.'

'We were talking about everything; football, women—usual stuff—and that's when it happened. I mean: literally, mid conversation. I froze rigid in my seat.'

'What happened?'

'I couldn't see Craig lying on the couch. There was a girl there, drinking his beer, instead.'

The inspector frowned.

'I did say this might baffle you,' Ford said. 'But, hear me out, okay?'

'Go on.'

'It was a girl, lying in the same spot, I mean, in the same *exact* way Craig had been moments earlier. She was young, early twenties.'

'Why'd you think he was a girl?'

'Soft brown shoulder-length hair. I mean I could even see the curved outline of her breasts through the purple strap top she was wearing. It was a girl, all right, Inspector. I saw her well-defined legs stretched over the couch, in just the same way Craig's ripped jeans had been before.'

'But you'd been drinking?'

'True, but not enough to Hallucinate.' He took his coffee in both hands as if he'd committed hence forth to being teetotal. 'Yet, there she was, right in front of me, sipping pale ale from the bottle. She turned to me then, with this confused look on her face. "What?" she said. Just like that. Only, *she* didn't say it, Inspector. The voice was low and deep. It was Craig's voice.'

'So, was this in your mind or—'

'Exactly, Inspector. I mean, it was!' He slammed the cup down. 'Like you, I figured it must be the beer. What else, right? Once the effect wore off, so would the hallucination. And that's exactly what happened.'

'She was Craig again?'

'Yes, after a few minutes. I pretended like nothing had happened. I suppose nothing had.'

The inspector splayed his large hands. 'And then?'

'And then, once the game finished, we went down to the local for a few more. I told him I didn't want to; that I'd had quite enough for one night. But I went anyway. And walking up the street, all he did was talk about this girl who worked behind the bar; this girl with incredible legs.'

'It sounded like the girl on your couch, right?'

'It *was* the girl on my couch, Inspector. She was even wearing the same raunchy strap top and short skirt.'

The inspector sipped his coffee. 'Your friend, Craig, couldn't he have mentioned her earlier in the evening? I mean, without you even realising it?'

'Maybe,' said Ford, 'but if he did, he described her too well. I mean, I even saw the tiny little hairs on her top lip, and I'm pretty sure no one with a crush would mention that!'

'Could you have seen her at the pub before? So, when Craig described her, you just brought her up in your mind…on your couch?'

Ford considered this for a moment and then said, 'Possible. But, a few weeks later, it happened again. I was

coming home from work—a shortcut through the park—
when I saw a man and woman walking towards me, arm in
arm. As I looked more closely, the man...changed. I mean
it was almost comical, because he morphed to match her
exactly. Like seeing twins walking along together. And it
occurred to me then, that this was the girl of *his* fancy. Just
as Craig's fancy was the girl who worked behind the bar.
That was the link.'

'But can you be sure it *wasn't* twins? I mean, isn't that
the more likely? If not twins, then, just two similar looking
women out on a stroll? At a glance, it would be hard to tell
the difference?'

'If these were two single occurrences, I'd agree. But
they're not. It keeps happening.' He put his hands to his
face. 'And it gets worse.'

The Inspector's chair squawked as he leaned back. 'Go
on.'

'I was at the supermarket a few weeks ago, chatting
with the cashier, when he suddenly changed! Jesus Christ,
I nearly hit the roof, because this time it wasn't the girl of
his fancy...' He shook his head, purposely. 'It was a
young, fair-haired boy. The soup fell out of my hands,
exploded on the floor, and this...boy, said. "Whoops," in
this shaky, gravelly old-man voice. I could hardly give him
the money before I got the hell out of there. Haven't been
back since.'

The inspector stroked his chiselled jaw.

Ford went on, 'I knew I needed to speak to somebody.
It was becoming too much. The first person I tried was
Craig. He'd been there the night it started, after all? But as
I pulled up to his drive, I saw two policemen putting him
in the back of a car. You, Inspector, *you* followed them

out. So, I put my foot down and kept on driving.'

'Wait a minute.' The inspector sat up. 'Are we talking about Craig Chamberlain?'

Ford nodded. 'Yes!'

'Six years for manslaughter.'

'That's right, for killing the girl who worked behind the bar—'

'Miriam Drake,' the inspector nodded. 'He got aggressive with her after she turned him down. Ended up dying in hospital with a fractured skull. Craig was lucky to get away with manslaughter.'

Ford raised his eyebrows. 'Remember the couple I saw in the park?'

'Yes.'

'The name David Coombes mean anything to you?'

'David Coombes?' The inspector thought for a moment. 'Sent down for killing his wife.'

'Found out she was cheating,' Ford said. 'Every time I see someone change; I see the person about to die. I can give you countless other examples and I'm never wrong.' He leaned forward and whispered: 'So, if any young fair-haired boys in the area go missing, you'll want to question the old man at the supermarket.'

The inspector studied Ford's face. 'Do you happen to know who the boy is?'

Ford shook his head. 'I never know the victims. But I know the old man's name because I called the supermarket and said how helpful the old cashier was. His name: Richard Hessler.'

The inspector scribbled the name down.

'I try to gather as much information about these people as I can; where they live, family members, local hangouts, anything. Mostly, it's too late, and all I can do is take clippings from the published newspaper articles.'

'Would you be able to hand this information over?' the inspector said. 'It may be of some use to us.'

'Actually, I already handed it over last night.'

'You did?' The inspector frowned. 'Then why call this meeting with me this morning?'

'It was the Chief Inspector's idea, a good way to keep you from the house while they searched it. I expect they've found what they're looking for by now, wouldn't you say?'

The inspector seemed momentarily startled, glancing back at the door as if someone may rush in at any moment, then to the tape machine reeling away with the Record button firmly depressed. Finally, he looked down at his large hands, to the band of white skin that once proudly donned a silver wedding ring.

Ford leaned forward. 'Tell me, Inspector,' he said. 'How's your wife?'

The Lottery Ticket

Anne Mean

Stan glanced again at the ticket tucked behind the clock on the mantelpiece. He had a good feeling, perhaps this would be the big win he needed to fulfil his dream. He'd missed the numbers on the Saturday evening news but Janice would look it up on her phone when she arrived.

He heard her key in the lock. "Coooee," she called as she slammed the door behind her. Stan gritted his teeth, she did have some annoying habits but on the whole he liked her and was grateful for her help with keeping the place spick and span.

He had to admit life was a bit lonely since Gladys died. Everyone assumed that he wanted to stay in little council house he and Gladys had shared for 44 years but if truth be told Stan was ready for a change. Many of the other houses in the close had now been sold to young families. Inevitably they were wrapped up in their own busy lives, the sense of community that there used to be was gone. It was what Stan missed most, knowing your neighbours, chatting over the garden fence.

That was why he really, really, wanted to move to the new retirement complex near the High Street. He'd read the glossy brochure that had dropped through his letterbox one day. It all sounded perfect. A small apartment all on one level, central heating, a balcony to sit in the sun and a 'residents lounge' for coffee mornings and other social activities. It all sounded perfect but... they were for sale. Way, way beyond Stan's modest means.

He looked at the lottery ticket on the mantelpiece again. He couldn't explain it but he had a good feeling.

Janice seemed to take longer than usual to check the numbers, looking first at her phone then the ticket. Stan watched her expectantly. Finally, she scrunched up the ticket.

"Fraid not. Sorry Stan, better luck next week." She tucked a new ticket behind the clock and took the coin that Stan fished from his pocket.

"Now let's have our cuppa before I start on upstairs." He watched as her ample bottom, encased in pink leggings wobbled out of the room.

***

In the kitchen Janice straightened the crumpled lottery ticket. Quietly she opened her handbag and carefully placed the ticket in one of the side pockets.

Turning to the cupboard she removed cups and saucers and prepared to make the tea.

By twelve thirty she was on her way to her afternoon client. But first she would call in at the newsagent.

Pedalling leisurely, her mind on what a difference £930,000 would make to her life. She'd use a chunk to pay off her debts. Then she'd buy Wayne the latest Game Boy he wanted, perhaps then he'd stop telling her what a rubbish Mother she was. She smiled to herself. Perhaps she and her best friend, Stacy could go to one of those posh spa weekends, a girlie treat. Wayne could go to his Dads. Although she'd make sure that useless idiot didn't get to hear of her windfall, she wasn't going to give him a penny.

She turned the bike into the alleyway that was a shortcut to her next client. Mind still mulling over the opportunities such a windfall would bring she didn't register the sound of the bike coming up fast behind her.

Suddenly she felt a blow to her right shoulder that sent her bike hard into the wall.

She felt her face scrape against the brickwork then felt another violent jerk as her bag was ripped from her shoulder. This pulled her away from the wall but sent her and the bike crashing to the ground. When she came round she was in the back of an ambulance with a paramedic shining a light in her eyes and assuring her that everything was going to be okay.

***

Darren pedalled furiously out of the alleyway, narrowly missing a young Mother pushing a twin buggy. By the time he reached the junction before the park, he slowed down to a more decorous pace. Didn't do to attract too much attention. He entered the park and turned left avoiding the play enclosure. Heading towards a small area of bushes. He dismounted and leant the bike against a convenient tree. He glanced swiftly round, checking he was alone. This area was a well known haunt of weirdos and perverts. Swiftly he raked through the contents of the bag, pocketing the notes, coins and cards. There didn't seem to be much else of value but he checked the pockets anyway. Coming across the lottery ticket he almost ignored it but changed his mind and tucked it into his pocket. Back on his bike, he pedalled slowly to the nearby parade of shops. He fancied a Red Bull and a Snickers.

Outside the newsagents he left his bike sprawled across the pavement half blocking the doorway. He needed to keep an eye on it while he was inside, there were some right villains round here and he didn't want it pinched.

Inside the shop he sidled towards the counter, looking for the chalkboard where Mr Patel wrote up the winning numbers. Two seconds later he replaced the ticket in his pocket. It would be no use trying to convince Mr Patel he was 16, besides he didn't think Mr Patel would have that much money in the till. There was probably some other way of claiming winnings that big but he didn't know what it was. He'd have to think about it. His mind on this problem he picked up a can of Red Bull and secreted it into the inside pocket of his jacket. Moving into the next aisle this was followed by two Snickers bars. He thought about paying for them with the money from the bag but he decided not, he always got away with it.

He added a packet of Haribos and sauntered towards the door.

His path was blocked by two coppers.

Sergeant Willis was on duty at the Nick. Darren was made to empty his pockets before being taken to a cell as part of a 'Teach em to never do it again' initiative. He watched the Sergeant place everything from his pockets into a tray labelled 'Darren, Cell Number 3.' "You make sure I get that Lottery ticket back." Darren glared at the sergeant. "That's a winning ticket, that is."

"Course it is Darren." The sergeant indicated Darren should be taken to his cell.

***

Hearing the clang of the cell door, Sergeant Willis withdrew the ticket from the tray. A quick search on his phone and the ticket was safely tucked into the top pocket of his shirt. His shift ended, he made his way out of the police station.

At home he only had time to change quickly into his Rugby kit. However, before he left the for the training session he made sure he attached the ticket to the notice board in the kitchen. It would be safe there. Molly would be delighted, now they could afford that holiday in Tenerife that she was on about and install reliable central heating and re design the garden, the list went on but it could all be achieved.

***

Molly came in by the back door. Thank goodness, Pete had already left for Rugby Training. She could have a leisurely soak in the bath and think. Gavin was getting more and more insistent, she wouldn't be able to stall him much longer. The job offer was too good to be turned down. A two year posting to Singapore to get him acquainted with the Asian side of the company with the promise of a seat on the board on his return. Being the partner of a wealthy international businessman or the partner of a custody sergeant in a small provincial town? No contest really but... there was only one thing holding her back.

Dried, dressed and sitting at the kitchen table, waiting for the kettle to boil Molly's eye was drawn to the pin board. Was that a lottery ticket?

She walked over and removed it. A quick check on her phone confirmed that this was her lucky day.

***

Stan was sitting in front of the TV trying to drum up enthusiasm for his tea of lasagne and chips. He felt cheated, he'd been so very sure that the Lottery ticket was a winner.

The phone rang, he picked up the receiver with little enthusiasm but felt better when he realised it was his daughter. Her voice was up beat and cheerful.

"Hello Dad," he could hear the smile'. "Do you remember me saying the other day that I might go abroad to live for a while? Well I'm definite going but here's the best bit." She took a deep breath. "Those retirement apartments that you want to move to - well you can! You can have the penthouse suite if you like! I've won the Lottery!

A Familiar Stranger

David Pryke

It is the dead end of the year.

Swirling mist rides on restless breezes; shifts, settles and folds itself on the night. A sharp, biting frost waits in the darkness wherein distances are immeasurable, and yet everything seems close.

On the horizon, a faint and sickly yellowed glimmer, like a three day bruise turning ugly.

A large figure, tall, broad shouldered and stoop-backed, dressed in a black coat, makes its way slowly towards something dark upon the darkness. Something solid, something squat - what might be a wall, what might be a low building, housing what might be a faint light.

The figure approaches.

The mist shifts, revealing iron rails and the dark cut of a platform. The rails run straight through this insignificant and remote station that will be axed in the spring. Tonight, the rails are dead silent.

The mist closes.

The figure moves forward, reaching, at last, the meagre and mean buildings of the station: a small waiting room, an even smaller office room, one window of which serves as the ticket booth.

From that office, a faint but warmer glow, dull red, a wound bleeding, struggles against the mist that is curled around the building like a living thing, nuzzling against the window panes as if expecting to be let in. Familiar, over-curious and persistent. Feline in essence.

The figure, moves slowly, silently. It approaches with intent, with stealth, as if stalking.

Inside the office, reminiscent of the cab of a steam train, and too small for him, sits the Station-Master. The fire burns hot and red: the room is stuffy, over hot. The Station-Master is a tall man with broad shoulders, slightly stooped, and although uncomfortably perched top heavy on a hard wooden chair, he half dozes in the heat. His face is lined with age. His hair is thinning and grey.

At his side, on a table, a stained mug of cold tea dregs, a half-empty carton of milk, an opened packet of biscuits. His black leather gloves wait. On the floor, by his foot, a saucer, with a circle of milk poured for the stray cat that visits from time to time. A large black Tom, stand-offish and aloof like only a cat can be, it comes and goes as it pleases and he has not seen it for days.

The embers on the fire shift, but in his half-doze, he merely breathes a little heavier. He might have gone home hours ago, but he has stayed, because home holds no cheer. Home is empty: a poorly furnished bed-sit, a two-bar electric fire, a two ring cooker squeezed into a corner, draughty windows and a cold bed. His life is one of sad dull empty routine: rise, work, eat, sleep. But in the main, work, for in his life, the station is the better place: it accepts him more readily. It is his refuge. It functions to his touch in a way his stark bed-sit never could, for that place holds memories of all he would wish to forget; a failed marriage, empty years, a childless, loveless and lonely existence. Moreover, the detritus of a spiteful divorce, followed by serious illness; milestones marking the bitter journey of his life.

The tall figure, so much part of the darkness, nears. Its steps are slow and deliberate through the mist that parts a moment, then closes again.

Inside the Station-Master's office, the large clock marks the time in its slow tick and slow tock. The Station-Master shifts in the chair and settles once more, half asleep, cocooned in a warm fug.

A sharp rap on the window pane startles him awake. Turning, he catches a face at the window. But the glass, blackened by the winter dark, gives a mirror image of his own face, faint, pale, almost ghost-like, looking out, pinned against the stranger's face looking in. For a moment, the one superimposes itself on the other. One a look of fright and surprise, of shock, even. The other, blank and emotionless. Dead pan.

Then the face is gone, and, now fully awake, he rises, his foot nudging the saucer so that it judders a little and the milk spills. The brass handle on the door rattles and he watches as it slowly turns. With a slight shudder against the frame, the door opens. In comes a tongue of mist, and in its draught, the timetable notices on the pin board lift.

The Station-Master's heart races.

Against the mist and the dark, in the dim light of the room, a stranger stands there - broad shoulders, black greatcoat, black leather gloves, black boots. Distinctive of stature, but the face is expressionless, set with dark, penetrating eyes. In his surprise, the Station-Master has the idea the stranger is somehow familiar, known to him: face to face, they are alike; similar in frame, similar in appearance. They might be related, brothers even.

But he dismisses the idea. He stares hard at the figure before him.

You can't come...

There's a Waiting Room for...

Unheeding, the stranger moves in to the room, and the space available seems to shrink.

Look, I'm sorry, but...

The Station-Master half raises a hand to remonstrate, but somehow, gestures seem futile. There is a silent space between them which the Station-Master finds menacing - this is his domain, and the stranger an intruder.

Against any further protest, and in silence, the stranger closes the door and moves into the room. The Station-Master makes way: there are words he means to say, but they do not come.

The stranger stands before the fire and the red glow of coals colours his coat. Gloves are removed slowly and one hand warmed, then the other. The gloves are placed on the table beside the Station-Master's. Slowly, deliberately, coat buttons are undone and the stranger moves across the room to hang the coat on the spare hook: side by side, the coats are two shapeless quantities of black, but in that simple gesture, a claim is staked.

In the grate, the embers shift and rearrange themselves. A coal hisses. Tiny flames flicker as the fire begins to die. An awkward, uneasy silence pervades the room.

I'm afraid...

Ignoring him, the stranger gazes into the flames. The Station-Master tries again.

You can't...

The stranger turns dark malevolent eyes on him. The room seems to grow colder.

I'm just about to…

His voice sounds lost. He clears his throat.

Just about to lock up and go…

He glances at the clock, as if to reinforce his words. As if, without the clock his words have no real meaning. But the clock is indifferent, and ticks slowly, solemnly.

The stranger nods.

In the silence, the clock strikes each second a dull, dead thud. It is twelve minutes past midnight; the red second hand reaches the top of the dial and begins its slow sweep down.

The Station-Master and the stranger exchange a cold and empty stare. Around them, in the room, everything settles into one hard chiselled and concentrated moment; there is a chilling calm that is the blood pumping deep in the veins, the sickening tightening of muscles beneath the skin. Something snuggles itself like a cat between them.

Look, I'm afraid…

A cold stare. A moth flaps around the light bulb burning in the centre of the ceiling. It touches and beats itself away, touches again and beats itself away again: the Station-Master watches it locked in this hopeless struggle. In the room, the air grows colder still.

Really…I can't allow you…

The words stick: in a terrifying flutter of panic somewhere deep inside, the Station-Master thinks this might be the prelude to a struggle, an assault, a fight. The stranger stands before him well balanced, shoulders squared, boots akimbo. Eyes dead and intent. The jaw set hard.

The Station-Master has done some boxing in his youth, pushed into it by teachers, mainly because of his size, but nothing ever came of it. He has never been a violent man. He has never been a fighter like that, never had the inclination to harm another. You're too soft for this game, his coach once said. You don't have the killer instinct.

True: he did not.

True, he has always lacked real fight: over a painful two year period he watched his wife grow away from him and still he put up no fight to speak of. There were times he felt she was waiting for him to show what he was made of, but he couldn't, and months before she left, he was already resigned to losing her. Already resigned to her being gone. Already knew he had lost her for good. Or for bad.

Later, diagnosed with cancer, the chemotherapy was the real battle he faced. And he tried, tried his best. He lay there, weak and sick, month after month, apparently resigned to it, but in truth, struggling against it in his own, so very passive a way. With inner resolve, rather than outward aggression. With resistance, rather than attack.

For months.

And then, out of the blue, so to speak, came remission, and with it, overwhelming relief. You're clear, the consultant had said, with a smile that looked empty. And at the same time, he experienced a feeling, deep within himself, that he was not clear, that this fight was unfinished, and would always be unfinished. Unfinished and inside, waiting its time.

That was three months ago.

Now, looking hard at the stranger, he feels the chill of the room. It is as though, with the stranger, winter has been invited in. He shivers. At the same time, he feels a cold trickle of sweat run down his spine. He swallows hard and, with effort, controls his breathing.

Of a sudden, in the distance, the piercing shrill of a train's whistle splits the night. The Station-Master freezes. His breath is caught in his throat. His heart leaps. He shoots a look at the clock: it is thirteen past twelve. There is no train due. Not until tomorrow.

What..?

The stranger, with a glance to the clock, turns towards the Station-Master.

Outside, out of the fog, but closer now, a low rumbling sound gathers. The silent rails now hum. They tremble. Like a storm approaching; like thunder rolling in fast, the sound builds and builds until the tap-dancing clackety-clack rhythm shakes the panes of glass in the windows.

What the…?

Out of the night, out of the shroud of mist, as if summoned, comes a train. An engine and a single carriage. The lights in the carriage are dim, sodium-yellow and cold. The brakes hiss, the wheels screech, complaining, and the train slows to a juddering halt.

Empty.

A log on the fire sinks in a whisper, like a last breath. Golden sparks gently rise. Above their heads, the moth finally singes itself on the light-bulb and falls to the floor.

In the room, one figure sinks to the floor and does not move. One figure turns from the fire and takes down a black coat from the hook. One figure slowly shrugs its broad shoulders into the coat. One figure picks up the

87

leather gloves from the table and pulls them on, flexing its fingers for a tight fit.

One figure claps its hands together in a dull thud.

The clock stops.

One figure goes to the door, turns the brass handle and steps outside into the dark. The figure, tall, broadly built, stoop-backed and wearing a great coat of black, slinks into the carriage and takes its seat.

With a slow hiss of brakes released, and a squeal of steel wheels, the train pulls away from the platform. The wheels turn slowly, and then quicken, gathering momentum with every revolution, picking up a steady rhythm.

The station is in darkness, shrouded in thick swirling mist.

Into the night the train goes.

The mist swirls.

In the station office, the fire dies down.

Darkness closes in.

Mrs Salco's Bed

Ana Salote

Mrs Salco's bed was big enough for four men, but they came one by one.

Other people, she had heard, passed down a tunnel to some heavenly anteroom for their life review. She wondered if it boded ill that hers took place in bed. For forty years this dark wood frame, these creaking springs, had seen the worst of her.

She was horrified when Rufus came bumbling across the room. He wore shorts and a vest, and the bed tipped as he dropped one haunch on to it and moved towards her with a series of muscular contractions and billowing bloat. He breathed noisily through his mouth as he settled. Within four or five breaths he was asleep and then the snoring began. Mrs Salco lay rigidly on the rim of the bed and hated him.

Lydia Salco was Mrs Ryde the last time this had happened. Sometimes she would lean over him in the dark, her face close above his. 'Shut-up,' she'd say through her teeth, and again: 'shut-up, shut-up!' until she was shouting. Other times she'd slap and kick him. He would snort, smack his lips and close his mouth for a few breaths before starting up again. Then Lydia would get up and walk with her pillow to the back room. She'd squeeze through the junk, knocking her thigh on the hard angle of the sewing machine. Even there the rumbling reached her, and in the long arrests she hoped that his great chest would stay deflated, his breathing paused forever.

But Mrs Salco was at death's door. There was no escaping Rufus Ryde. She would have to hear out the night with him. The rip of the revving bike he held in his throat: oh what torment for a dying woman.

'All I want is peace,' she said.

A hand seemed to pass in front of her eyes in a gesture of blessing. 'Then learn,' it said.

She stared at Rufus in silhouette. After three hours she had grown accustomed to the snoring. It had become almost soothing, like a mantra, wiping out thought. At that point the picture came to her. It was Rufus at about the time she had ceased to hide the fact that she despised him. He still went through that silly ritual of sending her a valentine, unsigned through the post. On February the 14th she had picked up the red envelope impatiently, slit it with her thumb and glanced at the kisses inside – his kisses were formed like little fish swimming backwards. There was a gift, too. It was a beige sweater, good label, but beige. She was not a beige woman.

She had thought no more of it till now. Now she saw Rufus, coming in from work, looking around the hall, seeing the red envelope where she had thrown it down with the bills, and the sweater which had dropped behind the hoover.

His hurt blasted her; one of many, many hurts she had piled on him over the years. She looked at him lying there. 'Sweet, lovable Rufus,' she said, and leaned over him and kissed him full on his snoring mouth. He opened his eyes and they shone.

Bob came while she slept. She felt his hands on her thighs, lifting her nightie up above her waist. She groaned.

'Will you take me, Lydia?' he whispered in his scouse accent. 'Come on now.' He had a wife somewhere she knew, but she didn't dwell on it.

The street light filtering through the thin curtains let her see again how handsome he was: green-eyed with black lashes, no spare flesh on him. He was a man, a soldier, the one she didn't marry; charming, unfathomable, without scruples. He would stay a few months then be gone to

Cyprus, Germany, Belfast. When it was off with his wife it was on with Lydia Salco.

His mouth was on her. She had a great desire to fall open to him but she stayed him with a hand against his chest.

'Don't be like that,' he sat back, his arm across his groin. 'Come on Lyddy, I'm aching for you.'

A woman stood by the bedroom door, anxious and peering as though through a mist. Lydia looked her up and down: his wife. We could be sisters, she thought. She hasn't my bust and she's a drab dresser, but… something likable about her. Yet here was Bob; why shouldn't she have him in her arms one last time? But the woman, the woman bothered her.

'Can I give you some advice?' Lydia said with a sigh. 'Hold yourself straight and don't look so wet. If you don't respect yourself, a man like Bob will take advantage.' The woman didn't seem to hear. Lydia looked at her more closely. 'Ah, you love the very soul of him don't you? I see it now.' She took Bob's wrists, prised his hands away from her. She grew cool, cooler and purer. In her old body she felt a new, bright well, and her words came up from it: 'Take him, he's yours. I have no claim, now or ever.' She looked down at her body, and up at his. 'All this I deny.'

The other woman's face lightened; her shoulders relaxed. Mrs Salco lifted as though she had risen up a step.

Henry was next to come and lay beside her, as always a respectful distance away, like a rescue dog uncertain of its place.

Now what was she thinking of encouraging this one? She'd a lot of grey hair coming through at the time and her skin had started to sit loose on her. Who knew if or when another man would come along, so she had taken up with the builder.

'Lovely place you've got,' he'd said while replacing a rotting window sill.

She'd looked up at the narrow terrace of blackened brick, a yard of sooty weeds between it and the main road. 'Lovely, I don't know about that, but it's all mine.'

And it's staying that way, she'd thought. She guessed it was not herself but the house he cherished; always sanding, glossing, cladding, proofing. 'A little palace' people called it once it was done. Once it was done though, she didn't really want him in it. His lashes and brows and ears and the line nose to mouth seemed always powdery with dust. When he fumbled at her with those cracked and bulbous fingers she mostly put him off. Still the mood was on her sometimes and he went to it cheerfully, again like a dog given a treat it didn't expect or deserve. Afterwards she'd despise herself for her weakness and resolve to pack his things the next day. It wouldn't take long. He travelled light as though he knew he was only passing through. What she had to learn from him she couldn't imagine. Ah, that was it again. She couldn't imagine.

'Henry,' she said.

He turned, surprised.

'Tell me about your life.' She leaned up on her elbow. He lay on his back with his hands folded on his chest and told her about his childhood.

'Your dad did what to you?' Though she was dying she bounced up onto her knees and knelt over, looking into his face. 'No, don't repeat it. So young... and you ran away.'

'Never been back since.' He took her hand. 'Do you know this is the first real home I've had?'

Mrs Salco put her face in her hands. She'd thrown him out as the last coat of paint dried on her newly perfect house. Not long after, she'd seen a shape like his on a park bench, but she hadn't looked too closely.

'Henry,' she said. 'Whatever happens between me and you, there'll always be a home for you here.'

'Do you mean that?'

'I do. I've room to spare and we are friends.'

Mrs Salco was very light now, very floaty; still there was an umbilical something tying her to the bed.

Bennet Salco was the last one. Her bed had been empty for too long. She'd opened the door to him, seen the Bible in his hand with the yellow satin page marker, the leaflets underneath it, the brown jumper and tie, the whitish-blue eyes with their unearthly fervour; and she hadn't closed the door again. That was the first surprise. She'd let him in, listened, admitted that there was something missing in her bed – or her life as she'd put it, and that yes, she did often wonder about the meaning of it all. She'd accepted the leaflet and his suggestion that he would call back and see what she thought about it. They'd married at the Kingdom Hall three months later. But the more she studied, the less she believed that she was chosen to live in a primary coloured open-plan zoo in this life or the next, nice though it looked on the leaflets, so she decided to do Bennet a favour and enlighten him.

Lydia studied the Bible for a year until she could quote chapter and verse with the best of them, but she kept her thoughts to herself. Then one evening when they were hosting the study group, she had asked an awkward question. Bennet had smiled, patted her leg and quoted at her. Unexpectedly, she had quoted back at him. For every statement he made she had an opposing one with full biblical references. Bennet had drawn the meeting to an early close, but she hadn't let the argument drop, not then, not for months.

She wore him down and wore him down till the unearthly light in his eyes began to dull and fade. At last one Sunday morning she suggested that they didn't go to the Kingdom Hall, that they stay there in bed. He had sat on the edge of the bed with his head hanging, his Bible on his knees. She'd walked around, taken it out of his hands and put herself there instead. Now Bennet was here again, in her bed, with his broken faith and his earthbound eyes.

'I shouldn't have done it,' she said. She took his Bible from the bedside table where it still lay and opened it. 'Look: my words, your words; the words belong to neither of us.' She had used those words in a spirit of cleverness and competition. That was no way to get at the truth. 'Here take it back.' She thrust his Bible at him.

'It's yours now,' he said, walking away.

The book lay open on Mrs Salco's bed. One line blazed clear: '...and the greatest of these is charity,' she read. Light flooded her head.

The cords that kept her there in the sour sheets and dust snaked free. Mrs Salco got up from her bed and flew.

The Withering of Sunflowers

Carol McPaul

Olivia feels calm. Eyes closed, she luxuriates in the warmth of the bathwater as it gently washes over her, the serenity of the moment soothing her soul. Never has her little bathroom felt so restful, its simple décor and neutral colours lulling her into a reverie. It was a good idea removing Marjory's clutter from the bathroom before she got in the bath. Marjory's clutter. She needs to attend to it, but it can wait ten more minutes, and she closes her eyes again in blissful repose, pushing it from her mind.

But Marjory's clutter *is* waiting on the other side of the door. A jumbled heap of toiletries that Olivia has scooped in armfuls from the bathroom surfaces and dumped onto the landing floor. Lotions for every overweight part of Marjory's body, Marjory's intoxicating perfume, Marjory's lurid peacock blue eye shadow palette and garish crimson lipstick, together with brushes, sponges and various other implements that Olivia cannot even identify. It isn't like Olivia to be so disordered, but it was all in the heat of the moment and she'll sort it in a minute. In fact, she is looking forward to the prospect of a whole 'KonMari' day tomorrow, organising everything and disposing of anything that doesn't spark joy. Heaven. She runs the tap and lets the water gently trickle on her feet until it is too hot to bear.

***

Getting a housemate had not been an easy decision. She liked her solitary lifestyle. After her mother passed she had gutted the house, cleared out the chaotic memories of her troubled childhood and created her own happy space where she'd lived and worked in peaceful isolation for most of her adult life. But Covid came out of the blue and some of her regular bookkeeping work had dried up. Bills needed to be paid. The agency sent Marjory to meet Olivia. She was a single female in her fifties with a good credit reference, everything that Olivia had specified.

'I work from home, so I need a quiet environment during the day,' Olivia told her, thinking it best to be up front at the outset. 'I do like to keep a tidy house,' she said next, as she watched Marjory make yet another ring on the table with her coffee mug, completely oblivious to the coaster that Olivia had deliberately placed there.

'You won't even know I'm here! I'll be doing my yoga and meditation practice – you'll not hear a peep out of me, my love,' Marjory promised as she put her mug down, missing the coaster once again. The loud volume of Marjory's response was enough to sow the seeds of doubt in Olivia's mind, but she needed the money and it was, after all, only a temporary arrangement.

***

Olivia, wrapped in her white bathrobe, lines up the bottles on the bathroom shelf. Marjory's jaunty sunflower towel still hanging on the back of the door reminds Olivia of the day Marjory first arrived.

***

'These are for you, my love, to say thank you for having me,' she had gushed, thrusting the yellow flowers towards Olivia. 'Sunflowers are my favourite,' she went on as she crushed Olivia's tiny frame to her much larger one. Olivia, stifled by the cheap perfume and chiffon frills, was not used to demonstrative affection and withdrew from the embrace as quickly as possible while trying not to damage the flowers or seem ungrateful. She wished Marjory would not keep calling her 'my love' – it made her feel like a child even though they were in reality a similar age. An exhausting commotion ensued as Marjory heaved her countless bags over the threshold and piled them untidily in the hall. *There are so many of them*, Olivia thought, and as Marjory prattled on endlessly about her journey there, she felt an ominous sense of foreboding for the coming days. But the agreement had been signed, and so the two women were to be housemates for the foreseeable future.

***

Olivia places the sunflower towel on top of the pile of debris waiting to be sorted. She pauses to listen out for any sign of life but is reassured when she can only hear the gentle hum of the fridge in the kitchen. It is a gratifying silence.

***

The theatrics of Marjory's entrance had been a sure sign of things to come, and Olivia's peace of mind soon withered with the sunflowers on the windowsill. She wasn't sure which was the hardest to endure – Marjory's paraphernalia or her perpetual overwhelming presence. It all reminded her too keenly of her own chaotic childhood. Most days she followed Marjory's trail of devastation around the house, gathering up discarded clothes, shoes, keys, towels, coins, dirty mugs and used tissues, just as she had done for her mother all those years ago.

'Marjory, I've collected all your bits together for you to put away,' she said as matter-of-factly as possible, not wanting to make too much fuss so early on in their cohabitation arrangement.

'Thank you, my love!' Marjory was unperturbed, humming tunelessly, seemingly oblivious to the mayhem she had caused in such a short time and to the effect that the constant disarray was having on Olivia. 'Can I get you a glass of wine?'

'No thank you.' Olivia felt irritated partly because she had already told Marjory that she didn't drink, but also because of Marjory's drunken slur. It was the same blurred enunciation her mother spoke with after the second bottle of wine, when she would inevitably blame thirteen-year-old Olivia for ruining her life.

***

Olivia's bedroom is her sanctuary, its white walls having been her only refuge from Marjory's perpetual disruption just as they had been from her mother's drunken chaos all those years ago. For the first time in several weeks, Olivia has clarity of mind.

***

On the third Thursday after Marjory arrived Olivia broached the subject of the 'oms' for a second time.

'The chanting is really disturbing my work, Marjory.' She knew that she needed to be more forthright with Marjory this time. The little nook under the stairs was usually where Olivia spent her working hours poring over numbers, making sure every penny spent by each of her clients was accounted for with the utmost accuracy. But Marjory's constant noise had forced her to retreat to her bedroom to work. Although she could just about tolerate the tuneless humming, the frequent trips to the loo and the running commentary on the latest Netflix series, it was the chanting that she could hear from every room in the house that was breaking her spirit. If Marjory had seemed momentarily dejected when Olivia raised the matter again, the second glass of red wine soon revived her. 'I'm sorry, my love. The oms help with the toxins, but I'll try and keep them low.' The irony of this statement wasn't lost on Olivia, as she watched her reached for the glass.

***

The moonlight spikes the bed with shards of light. Olivia gathers her papers and her laptop from her room, excited at the prospect of reinstating her under-the-stairs workplace.

***

The coroner had recorded a verdict of accidental death due to alcohol-related intoxication. Only three people, including Olivia herself, had attended her mother's funeral. Over the years, friends and family had been pushed away one by one. When the police removed the body from the bottom of the stairs, Olivia was offered counselling to help her come to terms with what had happened to her mother, but she was uncharacteristically self-assured for an eighteen year old, and immediately declined the offers of assistance.

***

'It's fine, Marjory, I'll see to it.' Olivia absorbed as much of the spilled red wine as she could in the paper towel, then she sprinkled the carpet with salt. 'I'm so sorry, my love, it slipped right through my hand.' Olivia wanted so much to tell Marjory not to call her 'my love', but she still managed to keep it in along with all the other things she so wanted to say. She gathered up more of Marjory's belongings littered around the room and carried them up the stairs. Marjory followed. 'I really am so sorry, my love, I meant to put that stuff away earlier but I got distracted with the yoga and then I had a phone call from my friend David and then I looked at the clock... I just don't know where the day went...'

Stop talking

Stop talking

Stop talking

Stop talking

Stop...

***

Olivia feels calm, like a huge weight has lifted. She felt the same way after her mother went. The sunflowers are done now, she picks up the vase and empties the flowers into the bin, then scoops the last of the dropped petals into her hand. *They lasted a good while*, she thinks.

Dim through the misty panes… I saw him drowning

David Oakwood

"Bent double, like old beggars under sacks, knock-kneed, coughing like hags, we cursed through sludge-" the teacher, his voice well-rehearsed, was suddenly interrupted by a bout of coughing from the back of the room. He paused in his reading, looked to the culprit…

"Sorry Sir. I was just coughing up the fags…"

"What? I hope you aren't daft enough to be smoking." The boy laughed mockingly. Slowly, the penny dropped. "Oh. No, Bradley. Not fags. Hags. It's 'coughing like hags', old women, a hag is like a witch. The poet…" The boy coughed again; he never knew when a joke had gotten old.

"Jesus! Shut up Brad. I don't want to miss any breaktime…" Izzi turned her orange peel face to stare back at the boy two rows behind her. The ponytail on top of her head was pulled so tight that there was very little room between her hairline and her pencilled eyebrows.

"Take your feet off the table please Bradley and put all four legs of that chair on the floor. *'till on the haunting flares…"* he continued, *"we turned our backs, and towards our distant rest began to trudge. Men marched asleep..."*

A tall boy, his greasy hair hiding his right eye, threw his hand into the air, distracting the teacher from the side of the classroom.

"Yes Jonathan?" There was a faintly concealed tone of frustration in the teacher's voice. Hardly the moment for questions.

"Er- How did they march if they were asleep?"

"Well, I suppose it is the poet's way of suggesting that the men were exhausted. Not literally asleep. Understand? So, the writer is using what technique here?" Cynically, he knew that question was going to be met with silence.

"Can't you just read it Sir?"

"Yes Katie, I think that would be the best way to help us understand the poem, which is what I was trying to do..." 'Give me strength', he thought and reminded himself not to let 'Can't we just...Katie' get under his skin. "... but Jonathan's hand shot up..." he continued, "and I thought it might be important. We will discuss the poem when I've read it all, but if you have any ideas or questions, write them on your copy of the poem. Okay?" He looked at Jonathan then, and the boy looked down at his feet. He hadn't intended to embarrass him. Poor Jonathan. So keen. So consistently clueless. Be kinder to Jonathan, he told himself.

"Ummm... I don't have a copy." Said Izzi, "I was sharing with Lexie." Lexie was a carbon copy of her best friend, and if Izzi hadn't been so mouthy, most teachers would never have learned which one was which. Their overdone foundation, a teenage camouflage, certainly helped to blur the lines between them.

"Okay. I have some more copies..." Sighing, he walked towards his desk. That was when the ball of paper hit the back of his head. He stopped in his tracks. Said nothing. Took a deep breath and decided to ignore it. It was probably meant for Jonathan anyway. He heard someone giggling. Sounded like Bradley. He took a breath, searched for a spare copy of the poem amongst the detritus of his chaotic workspace then turned to look at the class. "Here..." he said, handing Izzi a crumpled copy. "Right then. Do we all have a copy now? It would be good to finish this before the bell goes really, or, as Izzi already reminded us, it will be your breaktime you lose…" He took a long, deep breath, as if about to walk into conflict. *"Men marched asleep…"* He heard an exaggerated yawn but ignored it. Sounded like Bradley, again. *"Many had lost their boots. But limped on… Drunk with fatigue; deaf even to the hoots of gas-shells…"* He looked around the room. You couldn't take your eye off this lot for a second, but he noticed that some of them appeared to be reading it. That's a win, he thought. Probably because he'd said 'drunk'! He was exhausted, and he could tell they were bored. He needed to inject some passion into it. He knew how to perform this poem. Had loved this poem since Mr Brown taught it to him in 1986. Mr Brown, and the War poets, were the very reasons he was stood here now trying to drag this lot out of the sludge of ignorance. He exploded like a shell. *"Gas! GAS! Quick, boys!—An ecstasy of fumbling-"*

"My brother can get you some ecstasy if you want some Sir."

The class was a deafening salvo of laughter. The teacher braced against the onslaught, a true professional, swallowing shrapnel swear words he dare not speak. So, he glared at them all.

"Very mature, as usual, Class. Don't encourage him. Do you think… Sshhh you lot… Calm down! Do you think Bradley, I could finish this incredibly important example of English literature, and do you think, Bradley, that you could show some respect to the poet, if not me, just for a minute?" He didn't wait for an answer but drowned out the last of the giggling with a raised voice. *"FITTING THE CLUMSY HELMETS just in time…"*

"Helmets? What, like a bell-end?" Bradley. Bradley. Always bloody Bradley.

"Get out Bradley! Go on – you're disturbing everybody in here. Go and stand in the corridor!" He walked to the door, held it wide open, staring into the eyes of Bradley as he did so. Challenging the boy to dare refuse to leave. He thought, not for the first time, that those piggy little eyes were far too close together. Bradley, who'd just been awarded exactly what he wanted, tore what was left of his poem in half and threw it into the air as he toppled his chair, jumped over it and ran off down the corridor. The teacher then turned back to his class and muttered "Bell-end" too loudly under his breath.

"I 'eard that Sir. You called him a bell-end."

"Did I Izzi? I don't think I did."

"I 'eard you!" But she was smiling and didn't really care. She muttered to Lexie that she thought Bradley was a 'total bell-end' anyway. Lexie agreed.

"But someone still was yelling out and stumbling, And flound'ring like a man in fire or lime. —" the teacher had just carried on. The students looked down at the poem, something about his tone of voice suggested it would be better not to stick their heads over the top of the trench...

"Dim through the misty panes and thick green light, as under a green sea, I saw him drowning." He continued, but at that very moment Bradley reappeared in the small square window in the door. He pushed his nose up against it and left a trail of snot amongst the years of cellotape that had never been removed from the glass. No one laughed at him. He looked around, appealing for rebellion in the ranks, but they were bored of him. Just wanted to hear the rest of the poem, to get it over with, go to break and forget

104

about dead soldiers and Wilfred Sodding Owen and his miserable poem about hags and lost boots and lime and gas and ecstasy.

Annoyed that the boy had returned to disturb his reading again, the teacher repeated the line, *"DIM THROUGH THE MISTY PANES AND THICK GREEN LIGHT, AS UNDER A GREEN SEA, I SAW HIM DROWNING."* Now he had their attention. They could sense the emotion of the line in his voice. He was feeling it. His voice cracking with it. That's when Bradley burst back in… sauntered towards his chair, casually picked it up, sat down and instantly rocked back onto two legs as his scuffed-up muddy trainers thumped onto the desk in front of him. The teacher walked towards him, still reading, *"In all my dreams before my helpless sight, he plunges at me, GUTTERING, CHOKING, DROWNING…"* He passed Bradley the copy he'd been reading from and began reciting it from memory, *"If in some smothering dreams, you too could pace behind the wagon that we flung him in, and watch the white eyes writhing in his face, his hanging face, like a devil's sick of sin;* (He spat that bit towards Bradley) *If you could hear, at every jolt, the blood come gargling from the froth-corrupted lungs, obscene as cancer, bitter as the cud, of vile, incurable sores on innocent tongues,— My friend,* (He stood beside Bradley then, looked down at him. The boy looked up, apparently silenced into awe as his teacher's voice broke with the devastation of the words) *"you would not tell with such high zest to children ardent for some desperate glory, the old lie: Dulce et decorum est pro patria mori."* He was panting with the exertion of his performance, with the exhaustion of the lesson, with his own vulnerable response to such highly emotive poetry.

He didn't expect them to applaud. He didn't expect

them to say much at all. So, he wasn't disappointed when they didn't but was, somewhat, pleased with himself. They were all staring at him, and he had, for the first time in a long while, grabbed their attention. They'd listened.

"What the fuck does all that mean?" Yes, he'd sworn but that was a question. Bradley asked a question. Engagement. In an ecstasy of fumbling for words, the teacher tried to teach.

"It's Latin, it means "It is sweet and fitting to die for one's country. Wilfred Owen is saying that it isn't. That it's a lie. That war is not glorious at all. And don't swear."

"It's Latin for don't swear?" Bradley looked particularly pleased with himself. Great wind-up.

"No… You swore. Don't say fuck in my classroom."

"YOU SWORE! Sir just swore!" The others hadn't been listening. As soon as his performance was over, they'd dissolved into chatter amongst themselves (apart from Jonathan, who sat alone and was writing questions all over his poem).

"He called you a bell end earlier too!" chimed in Izzi, a keen traitor. Lexie nodded in agreement.

"No, I didn't. I… look… the POINT IS, Owen is telling young men not to listen to the lies told by old men who want to send them off to war thinking it will give them glory… That's the point. Okay?"

"Was he a coward?" Bradley wiped his snotty nose up his sleeve but looked earnestly up at his teacher.

"No. He watched young men, his friends, die in horrific ways whilst fighting in World War One. He wanted to tell the truth."

"Yeah, but… If young men didn't go in the army

Germany would have won." Bradley AND Izzi discussing poetry. Victory in 9D.

"True. I suppose Owen wanted them to know what they were getting into. Propaganda - do you remember we looked at propaganda last week? - Propaganda did not prepare young men for what they'd see in battle. They thought they'd come home heroes from some exciting adventure. But they were often traumatized, severely wounded and mentally ill."

Bradley looked around the room for support and said, "Anyway. Poetry is shit…"

Boom! 'There it is…' the teacher thought.

"Why do we have to learn it?" Boom! Another.

"Poetry won't get us jobs." Boom! The winning cliché! "I'm joinin' up. Royal Marines. Just need PE. 'Face the unknown' it says in the advert. I'm not a coward. You don't write poncey poems in the Navy."

The teacher backed slowly away. He wasn't sure he had anything left to give and stared up at the clock. The hands weren't moving. The batteries must have died. He prayed for a fire alarm. He might even smash the glass himself. As he slumped into his chair Jonathan put his hand up. The teacher's right eye began to twitch.

"Yes Jonathan?" his sigh was palpable, like the last laboured breath of a fallen soldier.

"What does fatigue mean?"

Index

This book is made up of shortlisted work submitted to the Burnham Book Festival writing competition 2022.

Our thanks go to all the writers who took part and to all who supported our festival.

For more information about the festival or to get in touch, go to burnhambookfest.co.uk

Printed in Great Britain
by Amazon

78851603R00068